Dear Baba

By

Abena Bediako, LCSW

Leyla
Know that you matter &
are important! Continue
smiling & shining!

♡
Abena Bediako

First Printing: October 2017

ISBN: 978-1-387-30701-2

Contact the author:

abena.bediako@ymail.com

Facebook:
https://www.facebook.com/abenabediakolcsw/

Dedication

Ethan, Adjoa, Jahsir, and Selah. You are my stars. You help to guide my path and I'm forever grateful to be your mommy. I love you always.

Divine, your support and love is so appreciated. I am honored to walk a path with you. You are a wonderful friend, husband, and baba and I love you beyond words.

I give thanks.

Prologue

This story was birthed out of a desire to help heal our children and community. As a psychotherapist for over fifteen years, I have come to know that people are in pain. As children we often become forgotten souls who remain in pain unable to express emotions in healthy constructive ways.

Over the last several years, police brutality in the African American community has become publicized, to the point where we have become desensitized to it. Our energy is put into seeking justice and accountability for the murderers that often get off without reprieve. But what happens to the children of the murdered father, mother, brothers and sisters? How do they begin to heal through the trauma?

We all have the right to be happy and to live loving and fulfilling lives. The difficulty often occurs in seeking the path to healing. This book serves as a guide for children and anyone who has ever experienced trauma and desires to take a step on their path towards happiness and healing.

My fifteen years in psychotherapy has taught me that we all have the ability to heal ourselves. Allow this book to serve as a vessel to help guide you. Tap into your inner-most self, heal and find happiness again.

Introduction

When a traumatic event occurs, a 12 year old girl's entire world is turned upside down. Everything normal about her life has changed. Why her? Who does she turn to? How does she get through it? How does she learn to let go of the pain and heal? Journey with her as she learns to forgive, heal and live again.

June 9

Today I went to see this therapist named Ms. A. She has me journaling my feelings. What's journaling gonna do? Nothin! Talking to the school counselor ain't help. But I promised Mommy I would and I don't want her to cry or hurt anymore or have to come to the school anymore to have meetings about me. I sit at my desk and stare out the window or stare at my book. I don't know the answers when my teachers call on me. I just sit feeling nothing. I don't want to be there and I'm glad the school year is almost over. 7th grade has sucked. My Baba was killed! He was taken from me, and I didn't even get to say goodbye. I just want everybody to leave me alone.

June 14

So I figure once a week I'll journal then that's not lying and plus it's keeping with my agreement of Mommy and Ms. A. So today in my session with Ms. A she tried to get me to talk. It was a session with just me. Last time Mommy was in the session with me and I didn't talk then. I don't know why she thinks I'm going to talk now. I didn't feel like talking so I didn't. I just sat there. I played with the beads on my braids and picked the polish off my nails.

But I was peeping her office. It smells good though. It smells like flowers, like lavender and roses but I didn't see any roses anywhere. Ms. A has plants around her office and some type of incense was burning, maybe that's where the lavender scent was coming from. I sat there and she kept smiling at me. I don't know why she was smiling but it made me feel good. I didn't let her know this though. She has a pretty smile but I'm not going to tell her. She has different pictures on the walls of beaches and sunsets and people laughing. She also has these quotes posted around her office too, like "There's a purpose for everything." Whateva! Was there a purpose for my Baba not being here anymore? I don't think so. I also saw a picture on her desk of what I think is her family. They looked all happy and stuff. I miss my Baba.

June 21

Ok, so I went back. I gotta keep my promise to Mommy. I want to be a woman of my word. Mommy and Baba both say that you have to keep your word and plus I don't like when people lie to me so I don't lie to other people.

Today Ms. A didn't talk that much. She said if I didn't want to talk then we don't have to talk. She said we could play some games and listen to music. I was a little leery at first but she really didn't try to talk to me about what happened. I appreciate that because I REALLY don't want to talk today. Next week is my bornday and I'm feeling some kind of way. My Baba's not going to be here and I don't like it or want to think about it.

We played Uno while we talked about my favorite artists and how her music is old school. She tried to deny it but she knows her music is old. She laughed and was telling me how my music takes beats and stuff from her music. She played a couple of old school songs that kind of sounded like some of the music I listen to. I gave her that much but her music is still old school.

June 27

I saw Ms. A today because tomorrow is my bornday and Mommy rescheduled the session. I told Mommy we could just skip this week but she gave me that look and told me to come on. I rolled my eyes and sucked my teeth. Sometimes Mommy really gets on my last nerves. I really didn't want to go! I don't want to talk to no therapist!
Ms. A said she appreciated me coming in today because she knows my bornday is tomorrow. She asked how I was feeling about my Baba not being here in the physical to celebrate with me. What?! How does she think it feels?! Oh yeah she doesn't know..nobody does. When she asked me that, I looked at her all mean like and rolled my eyes. I wanted to cry and get up and leave. I had to get up though. I couldn't keep sitting. It felt like I was going to burst inside. So I got up and started walking around. I couldn't hear anything Ms. A was saying. It felt like I was going deaf or something and my heart felt tight and I felt the tears coming. I wouldn't cry. I was tired of crying and I wasn't going to let no therapist see me cry. I wasn't crazy and I didn't need or want her help. I just want my Baba back. I miss him. I've never had a bornday that he wasn't there and I don't want to start now. I hate this! I hate what happened! I hate my life!
I hate crying and I couldn't stop the tears. Ms. A let me cry. She handed me a tissue and went and lit an incense. After a while, she had me sit and she took a deep breath

and had me take one. She told me that crying was normal and instructed me to cry as much and as often as I needed. I guess I will since it seems I can't stop crying.

June 28

I stayed in my room all day. I read some magazines, drew some pictures and listened to music. I really like listening to Zendaya and China McClain. I also like Alicia Keys. I used to always listen to Bob Marley with Baba but it's hard listening to him now. It makes me sad and cry when I hear his songs now.

Mommy had planned to take me out to dinner but I didn't want to go. I didn't want to do anything but get a hug from my Baba and hear him say Happy Bornday but that ain't gonna happen. The police made sure of that. Ms. A had talked to me about coping skills and stuff but what's that gonna do. Nothin! I tried to breathe deeply but that didn't work. You know what worked was when I threw my picture of me and Baba into the wall. You know what else worked is when I tore my book up and ripped my ribbons off the wall. You know what else worked is when I punched and kicked the wall. AHHHHHH! I hate this! I hate this! I hate this! Why did this have to happen to me? Why did they take him from me? It's not fair. I'm so freakin tired of crying. I just want my Baba back...

July 29

I apologized to Mommy today for the way I acted yesterday. It was just so hard not having him here with me. I heard Mommy crying yesterday. I know she misses Baba too and it's not fair. Her husband is gone and she has to raise me alone. She has no one to share her life with and laugh with and go out with. None of this is fair. My cousins are coming this weekend maybe that'll make her feel better.

I like my cousins and normally I would be excited to have them come. We normally play games, watch movies and we love double dutch and racing. But I don't want to see them this weekend. I don't want to talk about Baba or have people looking at me all sad and with pity. I don't want anybody's pity. I just want my Baba.

July 6

So my session with Ms. A was ok. She asked about my bornday and how things had gone. At first I was quiet and didn't really want to talk. I kept staring out the window thinking about how my bornday went and how it would've been if Baba were here. I told her finally that I missed Baba. As I looked at her out of the corner of my eye, I saw that she was staring at me with a warm look on her face. She told me that she couldn't truly understand how I felt but she had experienced pain and losing someone and would like to help me get through it. This was different.

Most of my teachers and my friends would say they knew how I felt and they understand and blah blah blah but no one can truly understand if they haven't been through it. It would make me so mad when my teachers tried to console me. They don't know me like that and all they know is what they heard from the news of another unarmed black man being shot. I didn't need their sympathy. I was glad when school ended so I could get away from them.

I am starting to miss my friends though. Me and my best friend would always talk on the phone and do things together. We would be on the phone for hours talking about going to the mall or what we were going to wear to school or which boys in our class were cute. I miss her. Maybe I'll call her. I stopped answering her calls when Baba was killed. I didn't know what to say to her and it hurt so much to talk about it. I didn't want to talk about it. I didn't want to think about Baba being gone. I don't know how to let anyone help me. I just want to stop hurting.

July 9

So I spent time with my best friend today. It was fun until we ran into some other friends at the mall with their parents. We were laughing (I haven't really laughed in such a long time) and going from store to store and having fun. We both love Justice and trying on different outfits from there. I tried on this red hat, polka dot shirt and black mini skirt that was real cute. I didn't even try to buy it though. I know Mommy ain't going to let me wear nothing that short. Everything was going good until we saw some of our friends with their parents out at lunch. I got so sad and started crying. My friend tried to console me but I pushed her and ran away. How could he leave me? Why did he have to go? Why did they take him from me? Why couldn't he be here to take me to lunch? I hate them for killing him! They took him away and it's not fair! It's not fair! IT'S NOT FAIR!

July 12

I told Ms. A about my time with my friend and how my day ended. It felt kind of good to talk to someone about it. Whenever I talk to Mommy, she starts to look sad and sometimes cry. I can't really talk to my friend about it because she doesn't know what to say. It's always so awkward when she tries to console me or listen to my feelings. My other family members make me feel awkward too and normally I end up going in my room or leaving. Ms. A told me my feelings were normal and said it was fine for me to be sad and angry. She said it was ok if one day I want to talk about it and then didn't want to talk about it. She asked me to allow her to help me with my grieving. She explained that people grieve differently and it takes different times for people to move through it. She said there were some things that may help me get through it and she would teach them to me. We started talking about different coping techniques. She told me the next time I felt angry to go for a run or punch a pillow. I almost laughed out loud thinking about punching a pillow. I had already punched a wall. I wonder if she knew about that. Anyway, maybe I'll try it. We'll see what happens.

July 19

Well I let Ms. A know that I went on quite a few runs last week and punched a pillow. She smiled while giving me a high five and said great job. I looked at her like she was crazy. I laughed a little bit. She reminded me that those were the things I was supposed to do when I got angry. She explained to me that anger is a natural emotion and everybody experiences it. She said that if I didn't feel angry she would look at me like I just looked at her. I smiled. Ms. A also said that it's how you express your anger that's important. We talked about healthy and unhealthy ways of expressing your anger. Ms. A explained that fighting, hitting other people or even harming your own self is unhealthy. She said sometimes people lash out at others because they do not know how to release the pain they are in. I can definitely relate to that. I told her that I had punched a wall and yelled at my mom and did some other things. She said it was ok because that was the past and wanted me to continue to learn healthy ways of releasing my anger. She praised me for journaling and asked me to continue to run and punch pillows. I giggled and said I would. Punching that wall had really hurt my hand and I don't want to go through that again.

July 26

I saw Ms. A today but didn't feel like talking much. We played some games until the session was over. I spent the weekend with my grandparents and I got really sad. They had pictures of Baba up EVERYWHERE and I wanted to leave but Mommy had something to do and I couldn't go home. They were asking me how I felt and how things were going. I didn't want to talk to them and I didn't want to think about my Baba being killed and not being here anymore. Sometimes it's easier to pretend he's away on a trip. I started crying and then they tried to hug me and tell me it would be ok but it's not going to be ok. It's not.

July 29

Mommy and I went out to dinner to my favorite restaurant. It was so good. I love that place. It's an Ethiopian restaurant. We sit at small tables that are close to the floor. The lights are always low and there's music playing that sounds like soft guitars and stuff. And the walls are painted red, which is my favorite color. They have this bread called injera and it's so good. Oh my goodness. You use it to eat everything else on your plate with. You can use your fingers and they have this fruit punch they make from scratch that's so good. I was really enjoying myself so when Mommy started talking about Baba, I just started ignoring her. I didn't want to hear it and I didn't want to ruin my night with her by crying. I think Mommy realized that I was ignoring her so she started talking about something else which was fine with me.

August 1

Today they had a 3 month memorial for Baba. I had to go. I didn't want to go but Mommy said I needed to go. I don't know why I needed to be there. I didn't talk to anybody or want to be there. All people kept talking about was how Baba was killed and how nothing's been done about it. They kept talking about missing him and how the police took his life when he didn't do nothin. That he was driving home and was stopped for no reason and shot. I didn't want to hear that. Don't they care I don't have my Baba anymore and it's insensitive to talk about it around me. I matter. My feelings matter and I miss my Baba. Honestly, I don't care how he was killed or why. I don't have my Baba. That's what matters. My Baba matters. He matters to me.

August 2

I started crying in my session with Ms. A today. We were talking about my week and what happened. I told her about the memorial and started yelling about it. I yelled about the people trying to talk to me, about the people talking about my Baba like they really knew him and about the police who killed him. Then I started crying and I couldn't stop. She asked if she could give me a hug and I said yes. I couldn't stop crying. I miss my Baba so much. Ms. A told me, while still holding me, that crying was good and I should not stop myself from doing it, if I felt the need to cry. She said crying was part of the healing process, and it helps to let go of the pain. She helped me to calm down and did a deep breathing exercise with me. She showed me how to breathe in deeply and slowly and exhale slowly. We did this this three times with our eyes shot. She had me visualize love as I was breathing in and exhaling the pain I felt. She told me to look at it like the love I was inhaling was pushing out the pain and filling those spaces. I was able to relax but I'm still so sad. My heart hurts.

August 5

I was thinking about the breathing thing Ms. A taught me the other day and I tried it today. It was cool. I was starting to feel nervous and stuff and didn't want to make Mommy cry or get nervous so I did it and it kinda worked. I closed my eyes, grounded myself and took deep breaths in and slowly let them out. Ms. A says grounding is when you center yourself, relax your body, become in tune with the universe and just be, whatever that means. Anyway, I did the breathing and I felt myself relax. It was kinda cool. I've been feeling anxious a lot since the memorial. I don't always want to feel like that and I need something to help me.

August 9

I saw Ms. A today and we practiced deep breathing some more. We started meditating as well. She called it a guided meditation. She had me close my eyes, focus on my breathing while she talked about stuff and got me to relax even more. It was crazy. It was hard to really really relax and not think about anything but the words she was saying but when I really tried I kinda got it. She said we would do some more of it at the next sessions. She said she wants to help me have even more tools so when I go back to school in a couple of weeks I feel prepared.

August 16

Today was a little hard. I saw Ms. A and she started asking me about school next week and how I felt and I realized my Baba would not be here. I don't remember ever going to school without him being there. He would wake up early on the first day of school, make me breakfast and give me a big hug on my way out the door to catch the bus. So I kinda shut down (this is what Ms. A says I do when I decide not to talk to anyone and become super quiet). I didn't want to talk about it. I didn't want to think about Baba not being here. So we started talking about how to cope. I listened as Ms. A talked about the tools I already have like deep breathing, meditating, running and journaling. I shook my head from time to time while playing with my hair and agreed to keep journaling. We ended by doing a meditation in which Ms. A had me focus on love. I got sad and wanted to stop but I'm not a quitter so I finished it but I was still sad.

August 21

Today was the first day of school. I thought I would be excited to start the 8th grade but I'm not. I really didn't want to get up and it took Mommy a long time to get me out of bed. I could tell she was sad and it looked like she had been crying. She said we had to be strong and Baba would want us both to have a great first day back to school. Yeah yeah but he's not here I thought. It doesn't matter what he wants.
I didn't have any classes with my best friend and didn't want to talk to anyone else. My teachers were ok. They didn't bother me too much and let me be. I did see my best friend at lunch and we sat together. It was cool. We talked a little about our classes. She didn't ask how I was feeling and I was glad because I didn't want to think about Baba or the shooting and why he wasn't here anymore. On the way to the bus, I walked past the security guard and started crying. I got real mad and my heart started beating fast. I looked at him real mean like and wanted to hit him so bad. Why was he here and not my Baba? I cried all the way home and ran in the house and went to my room and slammed the door. I didn't want to talk to Mommy when she got home or answer her questions about why I didn't want to come out of my room. I just hugged my pillow and cried and cried.

August 22

I really didn't want to go back to school like really. But Mommy said we had to keep getting up and doing what was normal. Well it's not normal. It's not normal that my Baba was shot for no reason and he's no longer here. It's not normal that he lay there bleeding while the cops look on. It's not normal that black people are getting shot for no reason. It's not normal that I didn't get my first day of school breakfast yesterday. It's not normal that I have to see Ms. A. It's not normal that everybody looks at me like I'm crazy. Nothing is normal anymore. Mommy scheduled an early appointment with Ms A today. We'll see how that goes.

When I went to see Ms. A, she had on her sneakers and said we were going for a walk. At first, all we did was walk and she would point out a flower here or there or a bird chirping. We walked and walked and walked. Maybe she knew I had planned on not talking to her.
After a while, she started talking about love and how it can hurt so bad when we lose somebody. I tried to block it out but I couldn't. She said it was more than fine to not be strong and to allow yourself to feel the pain. I kinda looked at her sideways like yeah right. She said that we're human and and everyone has the right to feel what they feel. She said that if I didn't want to be strong then it was ok. I started crying. I just want my Baba back. She said it was good for me to cry and scream and jump and do whatever else I needed to do to release my pain. She reminded me though that it wasn't healthy to hurt myself

or anyone in order to release the pain. On the way back to her office, she had me stop and scream. I looked at her like she was crazy. She was straight serious. She said she screams sometimes when life gets heavy. She started screaming. At first, I started laughing like is this lady for real? Then I started screaming and screaming and crying and screaming. It's like I couldn't stop. Ms. A started hugging me and telling me it was ok. She gave me a pillow to take home and use it when I felt like I needed to punch something. She said I was to cry and scream as much as I needed and use the pillow to constructively release my pain.

September 6

I had a lot to talk to Ms. A about today. I had been punching that pillow like crazy. It helps too cause when I went back to school, I saw the security guard and wanted to hit him again. I wanted to walk up to him and punch him in the face but I didn't cause I didn't want to get suspended. But when I got home, I ran to my room and started punching that pillow like crazy. Ms. A explained that the security guard was representing the police in my mind who had taken my Baba from me. She said it was normal for me to transfer my feelings onto the security guard. She praised me for not acting on those feelings and thinking about the consequences and using my coping techniques to release my feelings. She told me that I may continue to feel negative feelings toward the security guard for a while and it was ok. I know the security guard isn't the one who shot my Baba but they both cops to me. With Ms. A's help, I was also able to acknowledge that there are still some good cops out there and not everyone is like the one who killed my Baba. She gave me a homework assignment to write a letter to the cop who shot my Baba and to write a letter to my Baba. She said for me to be totally open and honest and allow my feelings to freely flow. I don't know about this. I'll think about it. I also told Ms. A that I was thinking running track again. They've kinda already started practicing but the coach said I could still come out. Ms. A said she thought it would be a wonderful idea for me to resume track. She encouraged me to go out and be a part of the team again. She reminded me of my coping techniques and encouraged me to keep using them.

September 8

So I started back running track. Everybody seemed happy to have me back on the team. It felt good to be out there running again. I got a little sad thinking about Baba not being at any of my meets but it's OK, I guess. Mommy came early and was out there watching me run and stuff and that made me smile.

We went out to dinner after my practice. I told her about the session with Ms. A and how I've been wanting to hit the security guard. She told me that she sometimes wants to hit cops too. Wow! Mommy wants to hit people. That's crazy! She also told me she was fighting for Baba because he was killed and she was going to continue to fight for him. Me too. It got kind of quiet but then we started talking about Baba and what he would have ordered if he were there and how he would be proud of me for joining the track team again and stuff like that. We didn't cry while we talked about Baba. That's a first. Normally I don't want to talk about him, especially with Mommy. It hurts too bad. I think this is what Ms. A would call progress, baby steps.

September 13

Ms. A asked about the letters and I said nah I haven't started them. She said ok and that it may take time and it's ok. She asked how things were going. We talked about track and how I'm liking it. School is ok. I still get upset with the security guard but he doesn't mess with me. I still hit my pillow sometimes thinking about him. Maybe that'll stop one day too. Who knows? I'm having a sleepover with my best friend this weekend. It should be fun.

September 17

The sleepover was fun. We stayed up late talking and laughing. We did our nails and hair and ate popcorn and watched movies. We hadn't had a sleepover in a long time since Baba died. I missed hanging out with her. Her mom and dad are cool too. Her mom popped the popcorn for us and made pizza and let us drink as much soda as we wanted and stay up as late as we wanted. They didn't ask me how I was doing or nothing. That was good. Most times, adults be all in your business and wanting to know how you doing, how you feeling and stuff like that. I talk about that stuff with Mommy and Ms. A. I don't need to talk about it with nobody else. They did give me big hugs though and that made me smile and feel good. Next weekend she's coming to my house.

September 20

My session today with Ms. A was OK. She had me do this exercise on love. I had to visualize love and then write about it and how I felt. We then talked about it and how love is in everything and everywhere. I started feeling sad thinking about missing my Baba. Ms. A reminded me that it's OK for me to be sad and everyone's grieving process is different. We started talking about Baba and what I love about him. I started crying but I kept talking and I started smiling thinking about how I love his hugs and his smiles and how he would call me his princess and tickle me at night. I love that he would run with me cause Mommy don't like running but she likes to watch me run. Go figure. Anyway, I realized I love a lot of things about Baba. I miss Baba and I love Baba. I told Ms. A maybe I'll write my letter to Baba. We'll see.

September 24

I had my first track meet today. It was good. It felt good to have the air in my air and feeling the pavement under my feet as I ran. It's like you're free when you running. I came in third in the 200 and my team came in 2nd in the 4x4. We're pretty good. I was excited at first and then I got really really sad and started crying when I looked over after the run and realized Baba was not there. A few of my teammates saw me crying and came over and started hugging me. Normally I would have pushed them away but I'm tired of hurting. I hugged them back. I just want my Baba back.

September 27

I told Ms. A about my track meet. We talked about me winning and she gave me a high five. She likes to give high fives and it makes me smile so I'm cool with it. I wasn't gonna talk about Baba until she asked me how was the experience with not having my Baba there cheering me on. It's like she be knowing what I'm thinking or something. I started crying again. I told her that I got sad when I realized he wasn't there. This was the first time that he's missed a meet. He's always there. I told her that Mommy was there and I was happy she was there but it wasn't the same. Ms. A said she understood and talked to me about how my Baba is always with me. She said I could write to him and talk to him and how he's always with me in the spiritual. She explained that when people die their bodies die but their spirits live on. She explained how everybody and everything is energy and energy will always exist. I kinda get it. She said it may be helpful for me to meditate sometimes thinking about him and being open to feeling his presence. Not exactly sure what she means but I know how to meditate so I'll try thinking about him the next time I do it.

October 7

When I met with Ms. A and she asked me how I was doing, I confided in her that I was feeling sad and couldn't shake it. We talked about possible reasons why I felt so sad. I told her that me and Mommy were fine. I told her that I've been getting along with my best friend and my other friends and that was fine. I told her that track was going well and I was looking forward to the final meet. She asked me about Baba and I realized his bornday is coming up. When I thought about it, I got really really angry. Ms. A reminded me that anger is a normal feeling and everybody gets angry about different things. She advised me not to run from it but to embrace the feeling and positively release it. I know exactly what she meant. When I went home, I punched my pillow so much I got tired. Mommy had gotten me a new pillow a while ago because I had punched my other one until it flattened out. I then started screaming. Mommy came and checked on me and left after she realized I was practicing my coping techniques. I felt better afterwards.

October 13

Me and Mommy met Ms. A for a family therapy session. She talked to us about how things were going. She started talking to us about my Baba's bornday next week and how we would honor him. She reminded us that it's important to honor those we have lost as well as honoring our feelings regarding those lost ones. We talked about different ways of doing it and settled on having a small dinner with just the two of us, making him cards and making his favorite dinner. I'm going to try really really hard to be strong for Mommy because I'm already getting sad thinking about it.

October 19

So yesterday was Baba's bornday. Mommy didn't make me go to school and she didn't go to work either. Mommy and I woke up playing some of his favorite songs. His all-time favorite is Bob Marley's Redemption Song. I was able to listen and sing along. I did cry but they were silent tears that felt cleansing. I don't know how to explain it but it was okay. We danced around the kitchen to other songs while making his favorite breakfast. We turned the music up way loud like he liked it and ate waffles, hashbrowns, and sauteed spinach and sliced oranges. I like pancakes better than waffles but it was Baba's bornday so we made waffles. We talked about Baba and smiled, laughed and cried. Later that night, Mommy and I made dinner together. We had the kitchen smelling so good. I couldn't wait to eat and I'm sure Baba was excited about it too. We made him lasagna and salad. Baba loved Mommy's lasagna. For dessert we made strawberry cheesecake and it was sooo good. We made Baba a plate and set it on his altar. I'm pretty sure he liked it cause I could swear I saw some dents in that cheesecake as I was cleaning up.
After dinner I went in my room just to be by myself for a while. It had been a long day. There were a lot of moments that I wanted to cry and not stop. I think Mommy felt the same way but we didn't. We kept moving and would look at each other and smile. I had made him a gift but I didn't want to show anyone not even Mommy. I had painted a picture of him and me and put it in a frame. As I lay on my bed looking at it, I

started getting mad. I couldn't stop and control it. I started crying and crying and my heart started feeling super heavy like I couldn't breathe. I tried punching the pillow but it didn't help. I tried deep breathing but it didn't help. I even tried screaming but it didn't help. I threw the picture into the wall and it cracked and ripped. Mommy came in and started holding me when she heard me screaming. She rocked me and cried with me until I fell asleep.

October 20

I told Ms. A about Baba's bornday and what happened. She told me that it was normal and nothing was wrong with me. She explained that I was still grieving and different triggers or things will happen that make me sad or happy. She talked to me about why I thought I got so angry. I recognized I was mad at the officer for taking Baba away from me. Baba should've been home with me and Mommy celebrating his bornday but he wasn't and never would be again. I hated the officer for that. Ms. A talked to me about the power of words and how hate consumes the person expressing it. I kind of get what she was saying like if I continue to hate somebody then I put all my focus and energy into them and not into the things I really want to do. She suggested I write my letter to the officer and to forgive him. I looked at her like she was crazy. She reminded me that I did not have to give it to him and I could burn it or destroy it some kind of way after writing it. I think I'm ready.

Dear Officer,
You took my Baba away!!! He did not do anything to you. He was driving home to me and Mommy and you took him away. He is my Baba and I'll never get to hug him again or see his smile or hear his voice and laugh. I love my Baba and I didn't get the chance to tell him bye and how much I love him. Why did you shoot him?! Why were you afraid of him?! He was not going to hurt you.

He loved people and helping people. You did not have to do it...you didn't have to shoot him! You took him away from his family. Do you have a family? How would you feel if someone shot someone you loved and took them away? What would you do?

My therapist said it would be good for me to forgive you. How do I do that? I don't know. How do I forgive the man who took my Baba away. How do I do that? Cause I really don't know. I wonder if you have a daughter. If my Baba had taken you from her then she would feel like I do. My Baba would never have done that to you but I would want your daughter to forgive my Baba. I will work on forgiving you for myself and just in case you have a daughter. Baba would not want me to walk around feeling sad like this and hating people. He didn't hate people and I know he would be disappointed in me if he saw me hating you now, even after the horrible, terrible, mean thing you did to him. He just was not that type of man. He probably would have forgiven you. He's a better man than you will ever be. So Ms. A said I could make an affirmation, I forgive you, and say it over and over until my body knows it to be true...I forgive you.

October 27

I let Ms. A know I had written the letter to the police officer. She said she was proud of me and asked me how I felt when writing it. We talked about it and I asked her if I could read it to her. She said yes so I read it. We talked about forgiving the officer and how I planned to do it. I let her know that I hadn't fully forgiven him but I was kinda trying. I let her know I was doing my affirmations and one of them was "I forgive you." I told her I've been saying it a lot, especially at school when I see the officer. We talked about other affirmations I've been doing like "I'm healed" "My life has a purpose" and "I'm having a great day."

Ms. A processed with me how I wanted to release my letter. We talked about flushing it down the toilet, ripping it into tiny shreds and throwing it in the trash or taking it to a stream and throwing it in the water. I wanted to take it to a stream and release it. So Ms. A and I left her office and went walking to a nearby stream that was a little ways from her office. It was so cool. She allowed me to sit there until the last pieces of the letter had gone downstream. Once I could no longer see any pieces of paper, we began to talk. I promised to take back my feelings of hate and dislike toward the officer who shot Baba. I promised to love myself enough to forgive the officer so I could fully heal. I promised to let go. Ms. A asked me if I had written my letter to Baba. I'm not ready.

Nov 2

Today Ms. A asked me again about my letter to Baba. I told her that I'm still not ready. She said she understood and would be here when I'm ready to write it. We talked about school and how things were going since I'm no longer in track. She asked if there had been any incidents that have caused me any pain or emotion. I told her I still get sad sometimes but I'm working through it. I told her that I still do my deep breathing, and I write and still run, even though track is over. I like running. It clears my mind and it's just me by myself in nature. I get to think about things if I want. And if I don't want to think I can just run and run until I feel better. She had me lead a deep breathing exercise. That was pretty cool.

Nov 9

I talked to Ms. A about the incident between me and Mommy. The other day we got into an argument. She asked me to do something and I didn't want to do. She kept nagging me about it and I started yelling. I don't normally talk to Mommy like that but I was tired and wasn't feeling it. I was going to do it but she didn't give me any time. Ms. A asked me why I thought the incident really happened. After thinking about it and talking about it, I realized I was feeling some kind of way about Baba not being here for Thanksgiving. I had heard Mommy on the phone the day before talking to grandma (my Baba's mom) about what we were going to do for the holidays. Each year, we spend Thanksgiving with Baba's family and we spend Kwanzaa with Mommy's family and all of our friends. I heard Mommy telling Grandma that she still wanted to honor having Thanksgiving dinner together, even though it would be hard. I heard her telling Grandma how she feels sad sometimes and will start crying. She started crying on the phone and it made me sad. I went back to my room and started feeling sad and mad. I miss Baba and I know everybody else misses him too. I didn't tell Mommy I heard her on the phone. I didn't want her to feel sadder or think I was spying on her. Ms. A pointed out to me that I'm still grieving. She reminded me that it's a process and to allow myself and others time to heal. She also reminded me to be mindful of my energy and who and what I direct it towards. She suggested I talk to Mommy and tell her how I feel and why I got upset.

Nov 10

So I did talk to Mommy and I love her. She said she understood why I was upset and we were in this together. She told me that she gets sad sometimes and goes in her room and cries. She told me that some days are better than other days and she misses Baba a lot. She told me that's why she wanted me to have a therapist and why she has a therapist. She told me that it's hard losing someone you love and not getting a chance to say goodbye. Mommy said anytime I was feeling some kind of way to come and talk to her and we'll deal with it together. She then gave me a big hug and kiss on the cheek. We then ordered pizza (cause Mommy said she didn't feel like cooking) and watched a movie.

Nov 16

Today Ms. A and I played some games while we talked about Thanksgiving and not having a session next week. She reminded me that we would not see each other. She then started talking about how I felt about having dinner without Baba. I told her that I had tried not to think about it and really didn't want to talk about it. She kept prodding and finally I let her know that I had started pretending that he was still alive and he would be at dinner. I started crying and told her that I knew he was dead and would not be at the dinner but it hurts to talk and think about. She let me cry and release my feelings and reminded me to be honest with myself and allow myself to feel all of my emotions. Without looking at her in a quiet voice, I said I would as we kept playing games.

Nov 25

Yesterday was very very very hard. I kinda didn't want to go to Grandma and Grandpa's for Thanksgiving. I asked Mommy if she wanted to stay home and we could cook and hang out and relax all day. I knew she was gonna say no but I had to try. I knew I would have to face the fact that Baba was gone and really wasn't coming back. At first it was ok. It was a little strange walking in the house and not having Baba there. The house smelled good. Baba loved sweet potato pie and Grandma had been baking. I started feeling myself getting sad but smiled anyway and found a place to sit. I took my phone out and started playing games. That's when things started going haywire. People started coming in and trying to talk to me and asking me how I felt. Don't ask me anything. I didn't want to talk to anybody. Some of my cousins started talking to me about Baba and I found myself screaming. I didn't know where it came from or why it happened. And I was crying. My Grandma came running and just started holding me and rocking me. I eventually stopped crying and my cousins apologized. I sat outside on the porch then until it was time for dinner. It was turning dark and there was a light breeze. The air felt good and helped me to relax while I got myself together. At dinner, everybody sat at the table. I sat beside grandma. They were talking and laughing and it felt like I was in another planet. It was crazy. How could they be laughing when Baba was not here! Then someone started talking about what they were grateful for. That's a tradition we do every year. But I'm thinking what in the world?! Are you serious?! My Baba is gone and you're talking about what you're grateful for. Mommy said she was grateful for family and being surrounded by love. When it was my turn, I just looked at everybody like they was crazy and dropped my head. I think they got the point. On the drive home, Mommy kept telling me that it was OK and she loved me. Yeah I love her too but I want my Baba back!

Nov 26

Dear Baba...

Nov 29

So I just started talking to Ms. A when I saw her today. I didn't even wait for her to ask me how I was doing or nothin. I told her all about the dinner and what had happened and how I felt. I let her know I had screamed and scared everybody and didn't want to talk to anybody. She said she understood and made me feel normal. She actually said she was proud of me for screaming, even though it probably did scare everybody. She said it was good that it came out and I didn't keep all those feelings in. I then told her that I had tried to write my letter to Baba but couldn't do it. I really wanted to write to him but I couldn't find the words. She praised me for trying and encouraged me to continue attempting it.

Dec 7

I guess my session today with Ms. A was ok. She started talking to me about the upcoming holidays and processing my feelings about it. She asked me my thoughts about spending Kwanzaa without my Baba. I looked at her like she was crazy. What she think? How she think I feel? Sometimes this lady...Anyway, she said she wanted me to be prepared so I wouldn't have to go through what I went through at Thanksgiving. I kinda get it. I miss my Baba and want him back. Simple as that. I know he's not coming back. I've finally come to accept that fact. He is dead and I will never be able to hug him, kiss him, laugh with him, play games with him, read with him or anything anymore. And it hurts! It hurts a lot! So we talked about ways I could prepare so maybe it wouldn't hurt as much, like just me and Mommy doing things alone this year, making his favorite meals every day, spending time with certain friends and family. We'll see.

Dec 15

This week has been cool. I met with Ms A yesterday and the session was cool. We kept talking about the upcoming holidays and being mentally and emotionally prepared as much as possible. She told me that I may never truly get over it but in time I would learn to forgive, release and let go of negative feelings. She told me that I would be able to smile when thinking about my Baba and not become overcome with grief and tears. I trust her so we'll see. I'm not there yet but I do think some days it's better. I can think about him sometimes and not cry. I'm even learning to forgive his shooter. I still say my affirmations daily and I don't get mad at the security guard at my school anymore. He actually smiles at me and I've smiled back once. But anyway, I gotta decide what I'm going to make Mommy for Kwanzaa. Instead of buying gifts, we always make our presents and share them with one another. Maybe I'll make her a plant holder or a picture frame or maybe I'll sew her a shirt or something. We'll see.

Dec 21

So today was the last day of school and the last day of seeing Ms. A until the new year. Ms. A and I talked about the holidays and reviewed my coping techniques. She said she wanted to make sure I was prepared and could reach in my invisible bag and grab out different tools when I needed them. She's funny sometimes but I like her. She makes me laugh and smile. So I had to tell her what tools I had in my invisible bag, like coloring and drawing, journaling (which I do consistently I'm proud to say), walking and running, punching pillows, and talking to Mommy. Ms. A also suggested since Kwanzaa was very important to my family I could make each day special and relate it to something positive regarding Baba. I like this idea. Mommy said I could take a break from therapy since I'm getting a break from school. I'm cool with seeing Ms. A. I like talking to her but I'm also happy that I get a full break. I'm gonna sleep in everyday and eat snacks and watch movies all day. It's gonna be great.

Dec 25

Today Mommy and I watched movies ALL day. It was awesome! I missed Baba though. It's getting tough but I'm handling it. Yesterday I cried. I was thinking about him not being here today to watch movies with us and eat pizza and snacks. I tried to write to him but couldn't get past the first line. I talked to Mommy about it and she told me that she had also been crying and it was hard for her too.

Dec 26

Today was very hard. I woke up crying and wouldn't come out of my room for a long time. Today is the first day of Kwanzaa and Baba loved Kwanzaa. It was his favorite part of the year, other than my bornday, of course. He would talk about the community and helping and loving people. And we would always host the first day of Kwanzaa with our friends and family. Sometimes, there are community events and we would go to those as well.

Today in Kwanzaa is Umoja which stands for unity and it was hard to find any unity in the death of my Baba. Eventually I came out of my room and Mommy was there waiting with a big hug and kiss. I could tell she had been crying too. Her eyes were red and wet.

We had already decided we weren't going to go to the community event or have anyone over. When I came out we watched a movie. Afterwards, we ordered pizza. We figured Baba would be ok with that. It was his favorite kind too. It had lots of mushrooms, black olives and extra cheese. While we waited for the pizza to arrive, we sat on the sofa and exchanged gifts and shared what we were grateful for and how we've maintained unity since the death of Baba. I was surprised that I was able to list several things I was grateful for, like Mommy, my family, my friends, Ms. A, getting money from Grandma and Grandpa for Christmas (we don't celebrate but I'm not gonna turn down any gifts), and having a Baba that loved me. Mommy corrected me when I said that. She said Baba still loves me. She reminded me that he is gone in the physical but never in the spiritual. It's like when she said that I felt close to him again and he was there with us. I gave her my gift which was a skirt I had sewn for her, and she gave me a picture in this pretty picture frame of me, her and Baba. I had never seen the picture before. It was the best gift ever. She said we would always have unity in our family.

Dec 27

I figured I would write every day of Kwanzaa since that was very special to Baba and since I haven't been able to write to him. I figured it's kinda like writing to him in a way. Today is Kujichagulia which means self determination. We went to a community event and I stayed by Mommy's side the entire time. Some of my friends wanted me to hang with them but I didn't want to. It felt like people were looking at us the entire time and it made me sad and anxious. I started sweating a little and my heart was racing. I talked to Baba the entire time though which made it easier for me to get through. And yeah I know he wasn't really there but it made me feel better to talk to him and made me feel closer to him. So I was able to tell Mommy on the ride home that today I practiced Kujichagulia by going to the event and staying the whole time. I was determined to get through it for Baba, and I did. I was proud of myself.

Dec 28

Today is Ujima which means collective work and responsibility. Mommy and I decided to have some friends over and make dinner together. Somebody made roasted potatoes and vegetables. Somebody else made corn bread. Someone else made barbeque, and someone else made cookies. It was fine at first and then somebody started talking about Baba. I got real sad. I didn't want to listen or participate in the conversation but I was stuck and didn't know how to leave the room. It was like I was frozen and couldn't talk or nothing. I found myself standing there crying but I wasn't making any noise. It was kinda strange. But I was able to stop. I closed my eyes, took a deep breath and relaxed my shoulders. I told everybody I was ok and it was ok to talk about Baba. I couldn't believe I said that when it came out my mouth but it felt right. I smiled and everybody started making their plates. Dinner was good too. We gave Baba a plate and I swear he ate it.

Dec 29

At the Kwanzaa event there was dancing and a performance. I really liked it. I sat with my friends and we talked and it was cool. It was kind of like old times with Baba being there. Nobody came up to me talking about Baba and that was cool too. After the event, there were different vendors there. Mommy bought me a book which was about a girl going on an adventure to different countries. But I had seen a bracelet that I know Baba would have loved to give to Mommy so I asked Mommy for some money so I could buy it. When we got home, I wrapped it up and gave it to her from him. She started crying and smiling at the same time. We sat by his altar a while just being with him. I miss him.

Dec 30

Today I asked Mommy if we could stay home. I didn't want to go out and do anything with anyone. She asked me if I was ok. I was feeling fine. I just wanted to stay home. She said yes and said we could make dinner together and play Scrabble after dinner. I went for a walk before it was time to start on dinner. I thought about my life now and not having Baba around. I cried a little. I took deep breaths and just started to talk to Baba.

After we played Scrabble, we talked about how Kwanzaa's been so far and then we lit the kinara. While lighting the kinara, we talked about our purpose, which is Nia. We agreed that we would work on making our community stronger and helping to keep people safe by sharing information on police brutality and how to change the laws. I like this idea.

Dec 31

Today is Kuumba in Kwanzaa. It means creativity. I was actually excited about today. We always come together at a local community center and do cool art projects and eat good food. It's so much fun. I knew exactly what I was going to do. My friends were there and some of them decided to make drums, some made jewelry and some of us painted. I decided to paint. I painted Mommy and Baba a picture. I drew inspiration from the word love and my family and friends. It was an abstract picture with all different colors. It reminded me of birds flying in the sky and they seemed so free. When we came home, Mommy found some picture frames. She had also painted a picture. We framed them. Mommy took her's and put it in her room. But we hung mine up in the living room so every time you walk in the room, you'll see it.

Jan 1

Today is the last day of Kwanzaa. There's always a huge celebration in the community with good food, drumming and wonderful music and dancing. Everybody and they mama comes out. It's like a big family affair and stuff. I felt good about it and wanted to go. When we got there, I found some friends and went off and hung out with them. We always liked visiting the vendors and trying on the jewelry. We also like watching the dancers perform. Their outfits are always beautiful and their dances are amazing. But me and Mommy had decided to do something special at home after the celebration. When we got home, we lit the kanara for the last time this year and talked about how we felt and how much we loved Baba. We listed everything that we loved about him. I shared that I loved that he taught me to have Imani (which is also called faith and is today's Kwanzaa word) in myself. He taught me to be strong and know that I am smart and can do anything I put my mind to. I know I will eventually be ok but he taught me to always look within to find my answers. I love my Baba.

Jan 3

School started back today. It was ok. Nothing special happened. It was a little strange going back after having being on break. I see Ms. A tomorrow. I have a lot to talk to talk to her about.

Jan 4

I told Ms. A all about Kwanzaa and the things me and Mommy did and how I felt. She listened and asked some questions about certain things. I told her about not wanting to be around people and just wanting to stay in the house. She said that was normal. I told her about our friends coming over and making dinner together and how I cried and it was ok and nobody made me feel bad about it. I told her about the things I made for Baba and how I gave them to him and put some of them on his altar. I showed her pictures on my phone and she smiled and said I was a wonderful artist. I told her about me journaling every day during Kwanzaa and how it was cool and it was like I was talking to Baba. I let her know I still hadn't been able to write to him yet but it was kinda like I was writing to him during Kwanzaa. She said she was proud of me for using my tools and encouraged me to continue using them. She told me one day I'm going to go to write and it's going to be Baba that I'm writing to. Willfully she's right.

Jan 11

It snowed last night so I didn't have to go to school or get to see Ms. A. She cancelled the session because she said she wasn't able to get out of her neighborhood. She said she wanted me to be safe and to have fun. Man, the snow is awesome. It came up to my knees. It was crazy at first going out in it. Some of my friends came over and we had the biggest snowball fight ever. I fell down a couple of times trying to get away from them and got snow all in my coat and stuff. It was so much fun. We made snow angels and built a huge snowman. We needed a scarf so I ran to get one of Baba's ties. Mommy said I could get one and told me where it was. But when I got to her room, I couldn't move. I tried to open the drawer to get it out but it was like I was frozen. I started breathing hard and everything. I remembered I could control it so I started slowing my breathing down and thinking positive. I kept telling myself that I was ok and I was loved and all is well. Eventually I calmed down. I just sat on the floor. I wanted to cry but I didn't. I just didn't know what to do and then the craziest thing happened. It's like Baba came and gave me a hug and I knew it was ok. It felt so warm and nice. So after taking another huge deep breath, I got up opened the drawer and picked out the brightest tie I could find. It felt like he was laughing so I smiled and ran back outside with my friends to finish dressing the snowman. Mommy came out and took a picture of me and my friends with the snowman that I secretly named Baba. And then guess what? There's no school tomorrow so I'm bout to pack my clothes and go to my friend's for a sleepover.

Jan 13

The sleepover was amazing. We made our own pizzas and cupcakes and got to stay up way late watching movies and talking. We did our nails and talked about the boys in our classes. I had a lot of fun. We go back to school tomorrow though.

Jan 20

Today me and Ms. A talked about my tools. She asked if I was doing my meditations. Nope. I forgot about them. So we did a meditation together. It was different. She had me sit in a comfortable position, close my eyes, focus on my breathing and once I became relaxed, to visualize a bright yellow light gently falling over me. I kept trying and trying but my mind was not having it. I kept thinking about my friends and what Mommy was going to make for dinner and what I was going to wear to school tomorrow. It was hard at first to quiet my mind and not think of anything. Ms. A said it gets easier the more I do it. We'll see.

Jan 24

So today I figured I'd try the meditation. I came home grabbed something to eat (I was really hungry today. I didn't eat lunch today because it looked nasty. It looked like crap.) Anyway, I remembered Ms. A saying if I wanted to get better at it I had to do it. I figure it's like running. I've always been able to run but when I joined the track team and learned different techniques and stuff and ran daily I got better. So I sat on the floor on a blanket and closed my eyes and really tried. I don't think I did that great but at least I attempted. I think Baba would have been proud because I did it.

Jan 27

When I saw Ms. A today I immediately asked her to do meditation with me. It went better today. I was able to feel my body relax and I saw the light. I didn't feel it come over me or nothing but that's ok. I told Ms. A that I had did it at home and had practiced it a few times. Sometimes I want to go running but it's too cold outside. I don't really like the cold. So instead I've been meditating.

Feb 5

I was glad I met with Ms. A today. Everything was going well until somebody called Mommy the other day talking about the shooting and the death of Baba. She wouldn't tell me everything but just that the case wasn't going too well. What does that mean? I don't understand. I kept asking and asking until she said it does not look like the officer would be charged with murder. What! How could he not? I started crying and crying. This is not fair again. First he takes Baba away from us and now he may not get punished. What! Ms. A listened to me as I vented. She told me to cry and it was ok. I screamed that it's not ok. She agreed that it wasn't ok for the officer not to be held accountable for his actions but explained that it was ok for me to cry and be angry. She reminded me that I can control how I express my anger and asked me how I wanted to release it. I started screaming. Then when I was done screaming, I asked her if we could draw, which we did. My picture looks all sad and mean but it feels good to have gotten some of it out.

Feb 6

Mommy and I decided it's time we join some organizations working to change things in this country. Mommy told me that it's very hard for her sometimes too to deal with what's happened. She said she misses Baba every day and she was very angry when she learned of how things may go with the trial. I'm glad it's not just me. So on Saturday we're going to go participate in making brochures and pamphlets to pass out in different communities talking about ways of dealing with police in your neighborhood and what numbers to call and stuff like that.

Feb 12

I told Ms. A about what me and Mommy did and let her know she could participate too if she wanted to. She said she would think about it but thanked me for telling her about it. She asked how I was doing. I told her that I was feeling a little better but I've been sad and having a hard time focusing in school and stuff. She encouraged me to continue writing about my experiences and feelings and doing my coping techniques. She asked if me and Mommy were doing anything special for Valentine's. I explained that we didn't celebrate Valentine's day because we showed each other love all year long. I told her about how I would get just because gifts throughout the year because Mommy and Baba loved me and how on our borndays we would always do something big. This made me think about how I hadn't gotten a just because gift since Baba died. And if I haven't gotten one, then Mommy hasn't gotten one either. Ummm...I think I'm going to do something special for Mommy.

Feb 19

My session today was pretty good. We did some deep breathing, some meditation and played a game. It was kinda chill. We talked about my coping with Baba's death and Ms. A asked if I had written my letter yet, which I replied nope. I'm not worried about it though. It'll happen when it happens. Maybe I won't write it. Who knows.

Feb 26

Today I talked about what would happen if the officer didn't get convicted. Mommy and I have been volunteering with the agency to help uplift people and teach people about their rights and stuff. I kinda like it. I'm learning a lot and I know that Baba was not wrong, which I already knew. We have rights and stuff and the police or nobody has the right to mess with us if we ain't doing nothin wrong. I talked to Ms. A about what would happen if I was in a situation with the authority that caused me to be uncomfortable and nervous. It made me think about how Baba must've felt, scared, alone and not knowing what was going to happen. That's a terrible way to feel and live your life. You know that's actually not living. I don't know what it is but it ain't living, that's for sure. I've been hearing other stories of other people who were killed by police and killed by gangs and other people. It makes me sad to hear these stories and I wonder why we can't really just get along. Why couldn't that officer see that my Baba was not going to hurt him and see that he was just a man and he had a family and was loved. Why can't we see these things in each other? Why is there so much fear and stuff in the world? I was talking to some of my friends about this and they said I was idealistic. I had to look that word up and realized maybe I was. It means someone who has really big ideas and thinks anything is possible. I would rather think positive and live positive thinking that the world is good, even after Baba was murdered. It really does take a lot to hang on to pain, hatred and hurt. When it first happened I couldn't hardly breathe and I was so mad at everything and everybody but I'm learning the more I let go of my anger the easier it gets to heal from Baba's death. I know that may sound crazy but that's how I think and that's how I feel.

Mar 1

Today I gave Mommy a just because gift. I had saved up some of my allowance money and decided to spend some of it on fabric. I made her a pretty blouse and made a bracelet to go with it. I wrapped it in pretty purple tissue paper and kept it together with a nice bow made out of yellow yarn. I wanted her to know how special she is to me and that I love her. If I didn't have her I don't know what I would do. She was so surprised she started smiling and crying all at the same time. She said she's going to wear it tomorrow. Now that made me smile.

Mar 6

Today Ms. A and I talked about me running again and adding that back to my tool bag. I like running. It's like I'm free to be myself and just be. So I've started back running some but it's still cold outside so I haven't done a lot of it. I didn't want to talk about court tomorrow. I heard Mommy telling someone on the phone that it was almost over and they may have a verdict soon. So when Ms. A started talking about it that's when I started talking about running. I think she got the hint and she stopped talking about it. I really don't want to think about it. What if he is found not guilty? What will that mean? How will Mommy feel? How will Grandma and Grandpa feel? How will I feel?

Mar 8

Noooooooooooooooooooooo! How could they do this? How could they let him go? Do they not know what he did? Don't they know he took my Baba away. Don't they know. They don't care.

Mar 9

I woke up crying. I went to sleep crying. Mommy couldn't console me. She was crying too. I was so upset when the verdict came in yesterday of not guilty. It was like we were in a twilight zone or something. When Mommy came and got me out of school and brought me home without talking I knew something bad had happened. She sat me down and told me the horrible news. I remember screaming and throwing stuff. I couldn't believe it. They had taken my Baba away and they didn't care. Nobody cared about me. They didn't care and he was never coming back. Never. Never. Never. And they don't care. He loved me and they took that away. I couldn't control myself and I remember Mommy holding me tight until I calmed down. I don't even know how long that took. When she let me go, I ran to my room and slammed my door and started punching the pillows. I punched and cried and punched and cried until I passed out.

Mar 10

Mommy took me to see Ms. A. I wasn't scheduled to see her and I didn't want to talk to her so I didn't. We just sat there in silence. She tried to talk but I wouldn't even respond or look at her. What could she say to make it better. Nothing. There isn't anything that anybody can say to make it better. My Baba is gone and will never be back. I guess she figured I wasn't going to talk so she just lit an incense and started playing some kind of quiet music without words. She told me that it would be ok even though it does not feel like it now. How does she know that? She told me that she was here for me and to call her anytime I needed or wanted to talk. Whateva! Can she bring my Baba back? Nope. Can she put the officer in jail? Nope. So I don't want to listen to her.

Mar 11

I went to school today. I don't know what for. I didn't do anything. I didn't talk to anybody or nothin. I should've stayed home. The security guard actually came up to me and told me he was sorry. He said he heard what happened and he was really sorry. I didn't know what to say. I just stared at him until he walked away. When I got home, I went straight to my room. I didn't answer any of the calls from my friends. What could they say? What could anybody say. Nothing. I didn't want to eat or watch a movie or nothing. I miss my Baba and want him back.

Mar 14

I was supposed to see Ms. A today but I refused to go. I just couldn't and Mommy didn't make me. She tried but I think she understood. I did not want to talk about Baba and the trial or any of it. I'm tired.

Mar 16

Today I went for a walk. I don't know how long I walked or nothin. I just walked and walked. It felt like I had to get out of my head. I know that don't make much sense but it's how I felt.

Mar 17

Today I talked to Mommy about what happened and how we felt about it. It was hard. We both were crying and she hugged me and I hugged her back. She said she didn't understand it and could not give me any words to make it make sense or even make me feel better. She said that she was very angry and it was helping her to talk to her therapist and to do some of her coping techniques. She showed me some of the pictures she had drawn since last week. She had drawn a lot of pictures. She told me that she's been to the gym every day and working out helps her to release her anger so she can replace it with love for me. That kinda made me smile. I told her how I've been walking and punching pillows but I was still angry. She said she understood and it was normal. She said it wasn't fair what happened and that the officer was not punished. But she told me that it brings her peace knowing that we still have each other and Baba would be happy that we are still living. She also told me that it brings her peace knowing that karma is real and what people put out in the universe, whether it's positive or negative, they will get back. So she said we do not have to will the officer harm or anything and if I had forgiven him then allow that to be because he would receive his due justice and nothing could stop it. That made a lot of sense to me. I know about karma. Its energy, positive and negative. Whatever we put out we will get back. When I'm mean to Mommy or do something that I know is not righteous something bad always happens to me. And when I'm nice to her or anyone then good things happen to me. So I started thinking about what she said and it really did make me feel better. That officer is gonna get his way worse than what any judge or person could do to him. And Baba wouldn't want me walking around being all angry all the time anyway. I don't like what happened and I don't think I ever will and I'll never be able to change it or get my Baba back but I still have my Mommy.

Mar 20

I went back to see Ms. A. I apologized to her for not coming and not talking the last time I was in her office. She told me I did not have to apologize and she understood as best she could. I like that about her. She doesn't try to be anything other than who she is. She's real and I appreciate that. I told her about me and Mommy's talk the other night and she agreed with Mommy. We talked about energy and karma and she gets it. She encouraged me to think positive and keep moving forward, even on days that it's very hard to do so. She also talked to me about doing a gratitude list. I told her I'd think about doing one.

Mar 21

So I decided to do that gratitude list. I figured it couldn't hurt nothin. I surprised myself. I wrote a lot. I am grateful for a lot of things. I am grateful for Mommy. I am grateful for my family. I am grateful for my friends, especially my best friend. She was always there for me and even when I yelled at her and hurt her feelings, she didn't stop being my friend. Now that's a friend. I am grateful for having a therapist. I didn't know I needed one and didn't think it was going to help but it is. I am grateful for being on the track team. I am grateful for having good food to eat. I am grateful for being alive.

Mar 27

I didn't go see Ms. A this week because it's Spring Break and Mommy and I are taking a trip. She said it's a long overdue trip and we deserve it. I think so too. So tomorrow we're driving to the beach. I can't wait.

Mar 28

The hotel is amazing. There's so much to do and see and places to visit. When we signed in they gave us all these pamphlets letting us know everything there was to do. We have a room that looks out on the ocean and it is beautiful. Oh my goodness, it's so pretty. I just stood there for a second on the balcony watching these beautiful blue waves wash up on the beach. We are on the 10th floor which is really cool cause when you go out on the balcony and look down it's so far to the bottom and when you look out at the water it's all you can see for miles and miles. I'm so excited.

Mar 29

Yesterday we had the best dinner ever. We don't eat meat so a lot of times we go out we can never find anything that we really like that tastes good. But they have this vegan restaurant that is amazing. Oh my goodness it was so good. I got the mock crabcakes that tasted so good. Mommy said it tasted like the real thing. (She used to eat meat.) The sauce that went with it was delicious. I could've ate it all by itself. And then I got to order dessert so I got a slice of key lime pie. That place may be my new favorite restaurant. And when we got back to our room, Mommy and I sat out on the balcony. It was nice and peaceful. Today we did a couple of small activities but mostly sat on the beach and collected sea shells and read our books. I love the beach. It's one of my favorite places on earth. I miss Baba though. I told Mommy that I miss him and she said she did too. She came up with an idea that we should do a healing exercise where we write or draw something about our feelings for Baba and then release it in the water. I'm down for that. So tomorrow morning we're suppose to wake up and do the activity and then go to the beach.

Mar 30

Today was different. Mommy and I woke up and we decided to draw pictures. Mommy always keeps paper and crayons or markers with her. She's a beautiful artist. She said we should be open and allow our feelings to freely flow so we could release anything and everything that needed to be released. So at first I just sat there staring at the paper. I wasn't quite sure what to do. Then I started feeling all these feelings all at the same time which was crazy. I started crying and remembered Ms. A saying that crying was healing and to allow my tears to flow. So that's what I did. I picked up the crayons and allowed my feelings to flow just as my tears were flowing. I thought about how much I love Baba. I thought about how much I miss Baba. I thought about how much I am angry at him for leaving me. This caught me by surprise cause I didn't know I was angry at him. I had to stop drawing. I asked Mommy if I could write instead. She said sure so that's what I did.

Dear Baba

I love you and I am mad at you. You left me. You left me and Mommy all alone. I'm mad at you because you got yourself shot and murdered. I know it wasn't your fault but you still left and you're not here and you're never coming back. Why did you leave us? Why did you go? People keep saying it'll get easier and I'll understand. I don't think they are being honest. I don't think I'll ever understand cause it don't make sense. You're not here and you're not coming back. I have been very angry with you. I didn't even know I was mad at you but I am. I am very mad at you. I looked up to you. You were my hero and now you're gone. Why Baba why? Why did you have to leave? And I know I won't be mad with you forever because you are my Baba and I do still love you. I'll always love you. I love when you would read to me and tell me stories about when I was a baby. I love when you would come home and bring me gifts. I love when we would run together. I love when we would make Mommy surprise meals together. I love when something bad happened you would hug me and tell me it would be ok and I'd always have you to protect me. But you're not here now. Are you? Where are you when I need you now? I need you Baba. I'm your little girl and I need you. I love you Baba and I'm sorry that you were shot and murdered. I'm sorry that you're not here anymore. I'm sorry that I yelled at you and talked back to you and stumped my feet at you and hurt your feelings. I'm sorry that I was angry with you for dying. It's not your fault. I'm sorry Baba. Please forgive me. I love you. I forgive you for leaving me and Mommy. I know if you could still be here you would. I know you love me. I know you love Mommy. I know I will always be your baby girl. I love you Baba and I'm grateful that you will always be my Baba.

We went to the beach after Mommy had finished her painting and I had finished my letter. I read my letter out loud and Mommy cried as she listened to me. I ripped it up along with my picture and threw it into the ocean. Mommy said some words quietly to herself and then ripped her picture up and threw it in the ocean. We then sat there hugging and just being. Later we went and got lunch and came back to the beach. It's strange but it's like I feel Baba even more now. I told Mommy about this and she said she did too. That made us both smile.

Mar 31

Today was shopping day. Mommy and me both like shopping. Baba would find something to drink and sit while we shopped. It would always be so much fun. He would smile at us while we went from store to store. I miss him a lot today but I know he's with me. I can't really explain it. I just know it.

Apr 3

I returned to school today. I had so much fun at the beach. Ms. A would say it was cleansing. I would agree. I see her tomorrow. I'm sure she's going to smile and give me a hug or high five or something for what I did at the beach. She's funny.

Apr 4

Today was a good session. I told Ms. A all about me and Mommy's beach trip. She gave me a hug and said she was proud of me. I knew she was gonna do that. She said it was very brave of me to acknowledge and face my feelings. I never looked at myself as being brave but I guess I am. She suggested since I use my journaling as a major coping technique why not start writing to Baba. I kinda like this idea.

Apr 11

Dear Baba

Today I saw Ms. A and we talked about how things were going and how I was coping. I let her know that most days are good and it's alright but I do have days that I still get sad but the sadness doesn't last long anymore. That's a good thing. I think I'm healing. Mommy and I decided we're going to have a party this weekend for you. Yeah we know it's not your bornday or the day you were murdered but we think it's time that we start celebrating and honoring your life and having the family and all our friends do it too. Willing you enjoy it.

Apr 13

Dear Baba

Did you enjoy the party? I sure did. I had so much fun. The music was bangin. I know if you were here you would've been on the dance floor all night. I know I cried a little bit but remember crying is part of the healing process. I didn't cry long but I miss you so it's ok for me to cry. But anyway, did you like the food and drink we left for you on the altar? Mommy and I made it together. We did something different this time. We added 2 different kinds of mushrooms, artichokes, and 3 different types of cheese to the lasagna. That was my idea. Did you see all the people who came out to celebrate you? Everybody was happy and had such a good time. Some people cried a little bit when other people got up to share something they love about you. So many people love you. You are a great man and I'm very grateful you are MY Baba. I love you.

April 21

Dear Baba

On my way to see Ms. A. I'm sure I'll have a lot to tell you when I get back. Love you.

Tool Bag

*Screaming outside, in your room, or in the bathroom

*Running/Walking

*Journaling

*Drawing/Coloring

*Deep Breathing

*Meditating

*Yoga

*Affirmations

* _____

* _____

* _____

Affirmations

I am well

I love myself

I am worthy

I deserve love

I forgive

I am healed

I matter

_____

_____

_____

_____

_____

Glossary

Altar- a table or structure in which items are placed to honor our ancestors

Baba- another word for father or dad

Bornday- the day someone was born; another way to say birthday

Kinara- candleholder used during Kwanzaa

Kwanzaa- a cultural holiday celebrated for 7 days from December 26 to January 1

Meditation- a way to quiet and center yourself in order to balance and slow down your thoughts

Righteous- when someone or something is decent and upstanding; doing the right thing